For Louie Jarman, who makes delicious chocolate cakes and
Josh Pearce who likes eating them – JJ
For Davide, the magic kid – AG

Crabtree Publishing Company
www.crabtreebooks.com

PMB 16A, 350 Fifth Avenue,
Suite 3308,
New York, NY
10118

612 Welland Avenue,
St. Catharines,
Ontario, Canada
L2M 5V6

Published by Crabtree Publishing Company 2004
Published in 2001 by Random Houe Children's Books and Red Fox

Cataloging-in-Publication data

Jarman, Julia.
The magic backpack / written by Julia Jarman ; illustrated by Adriano Gon.
    p. cm. – (Flying foxes)
    Summary: Josh has forgotten the chocolate his class needs to make a
chocolate cake and he must rely on his magic backpack to pick up the
missing ingredient.
    ISBN 0-7787-1487-X (RLB) – ISBN 0-7787-1533-7 (PB)
    [1. Food–Fiction. 2. Agriculture–Fiction.] I. Gon, Adriano ill. II. Title. III.
Series.

2003022723
LC

Set in Cheltenham Book Infant

1 2 3 4 5 6 7 8 9 0 Printed and bound in Malaysia by Tien Wah Press 0 9 8 7 6 5 4 3

The Magic Backpack

Julia Jarman
Adriano Gon

Josh was having a forgetful week.
On Monday he forgot his reading book.

On Tuesday he forgot his gym shoes.

On Wednesday he forgot it
was a school day and he
was almost late.

Then he remembered
his magic backpack.

Useful pockets for
keeping things

Wings for
flying

Pull strings
to open
wings

Pull both strings
to lift off.
Let go of the strings
to go down.

Pull this string
to go East

Talking zipper
mouth

Pull this string
to go West

Josh's magic backpack was very useful.
It had amazing powers.

Josh pulled the strings of his magic
backpack and . . .

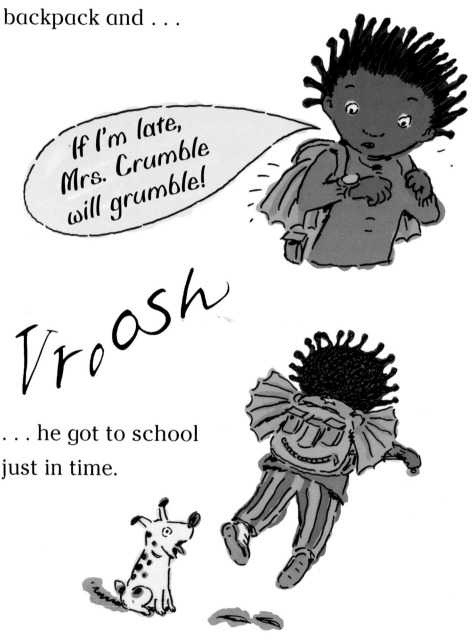

If I'm late,
Mrs. Crumble
will grumble!

Vroosh

. . . he got to school
just in time.

Mrs. Crumble said, "Sit down quickly, Josh. We are looking at this recipe and this map of the world. Today we will find out where the ingredients – the things we will need to make our cake – come from."

CHOCOLATE CAKE
INGREDIENTS
1¾ cup self-rising flour
¾ cup soft butter
¾ cup white sugar   3 eggs
1 level teaspoon of baking powder
3 level tablespoons of <u>cocoa</u> powder
4 tablespoons of warm water

"Tomorrow we'll make a delicious chocolate cake."

"Eggs come from hens," said Freddie, who
lived on a farm.

"You can bring the eggs," said Mrs. Crumble.

"Butter comes from cows' milk,"
said Katie.

"Flour comes from wheat," said Melanie.

"Sugar comes from sugar cane,"
said Nadia.

"Or sugar beet," said James.

Some sugar cane grows in Mauritius.

Some sugar beet grows in England.

"Chocolate comes from cocoa," said Tracy.

"My Uncle William has a cocoa plantation in Ghana," said Josh.

"Ghana is in Africa," said Mrs. Crumble.

"You can bring the cocoa, Josh, and the chocolate for the delicious chocolate topping. Please, please don't forget."

At home-time, Mrs. Crumble gave them all letters. Josh's letter said:

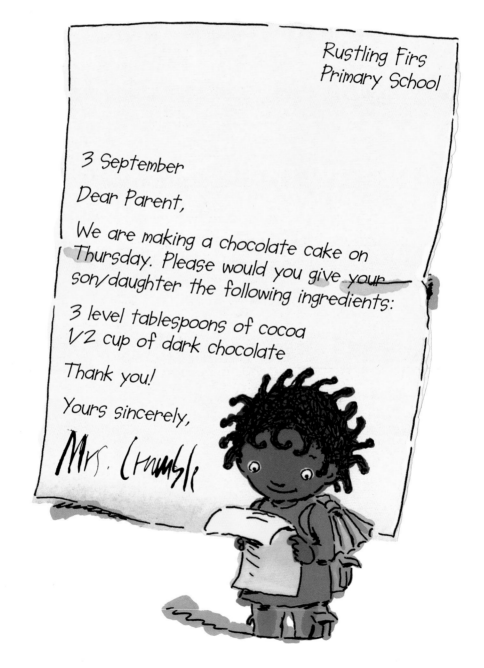

Rustling Firs
Primary School

3 September

Dear Parent,

We are making a chocolate cake on Thursday. Please would you give your son/daughter the following ingredients:

3 level tablespoons of cocoa
1/2 cup of dark chocolate

Thank you!

Yours sincerely,

Mrs. Crumble

Josh gave Freddie a ride home on his
magic backpack.

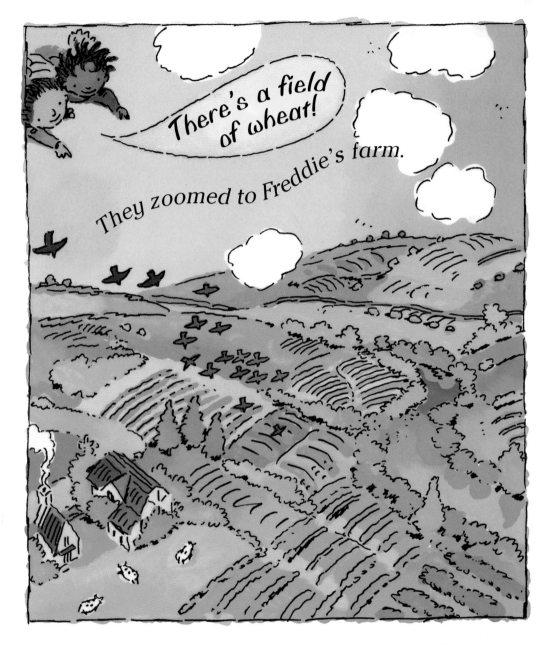

They saw a cow being milked and a hen
laying an egg.

When Josh got home, he
told his mom all about
Freddie's farm, but he
forgot to tell her about
the chocolate cake.

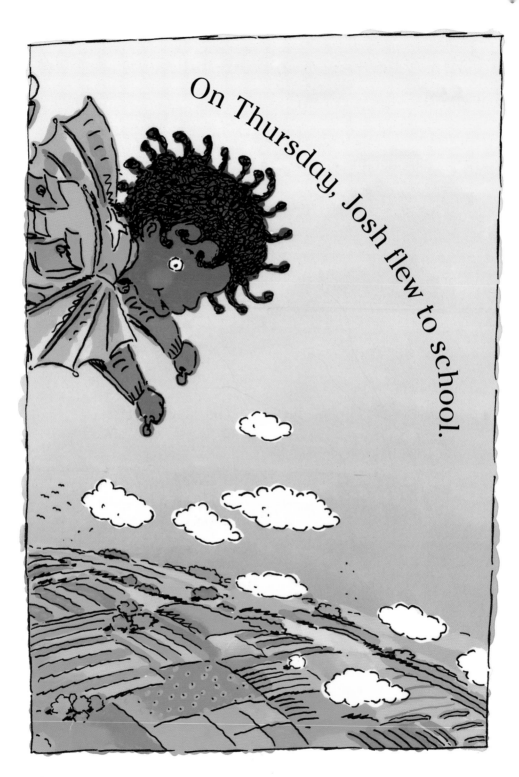

On Thursday, Josh flew to school.

Mrs. Crumble said, "Did you remember the ingredients, children?"

Freddie had the eggs.

Katie had the butter.

Melanie had the flour.

James had the sugar, but Josh had forgotten the cocoa and the chocolate for the delicious chocolate topping.

Everyone was upset with Josh – except Tracy.

It was a mistake!

Mrs. Crumble grumbled, "After recess we will make a cake, but it won't be a chocolate cake."

Josh had to stay in at recess. Poor Josh. He was angry with himself. "Why? Why am I so forgetful?" he said aloud. Then he heard a voice:

Josh! Josh! Don't delay! Pull on my strings to save the day!

It was his magic backpack. He had forgotten about that, too. Josh pulled the strings.

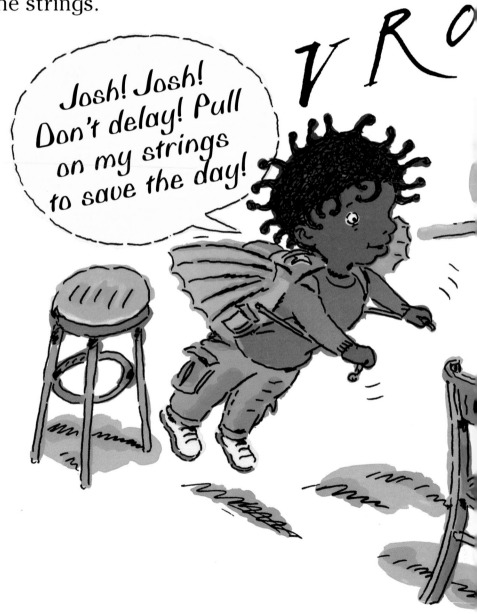

Josh! Josh! Don't delay! Pull on my strings to save the day!

ooosh!

His feet left
the ground.

He flew through
the window into
the playground.
"Wait for me!"
said Tracy,
grabbing
his legs.

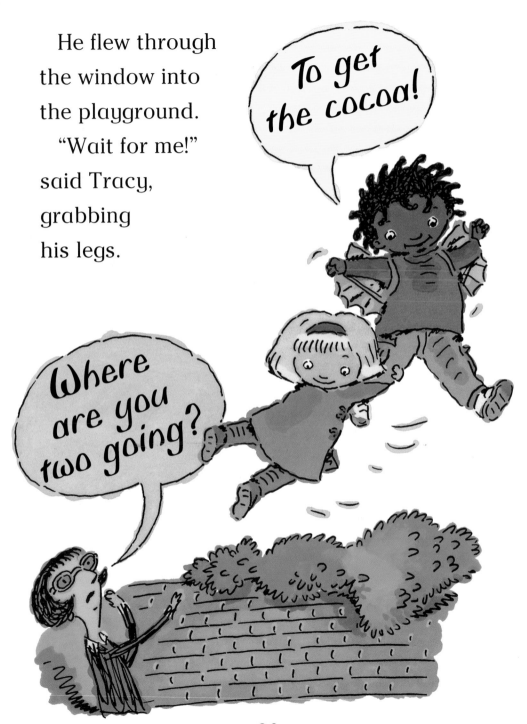

To get the cocoa!

Where are you two going?

Josh thought he was going home, or to
the store, but they flew over his house,
and over the store. They left their town
behind them and the next town too.

Suddenly they were flying over the sea!
Josh had never flown so far – or so fast.

"Where are we going?" gasped Tracy.

"To Africa, I think."

"But that's thousands of miles. It will take
hours," said Tracy.

"I hope not," said Josh.

They whizzed over France and Spain, and over the Mediterranean Sea.

"We're over Africa now!" said Tracy. "There's desert below."

"And rainforest ahead," said Josh.

He saw a cocoa plantation and let go of the magic backpack strings.

"Hello, Josh!" said Uncle William.

"Hello, Uncle William," said Josh.

"I need some cocoa and some chocolate, please."

Goodness me, it's Josh!

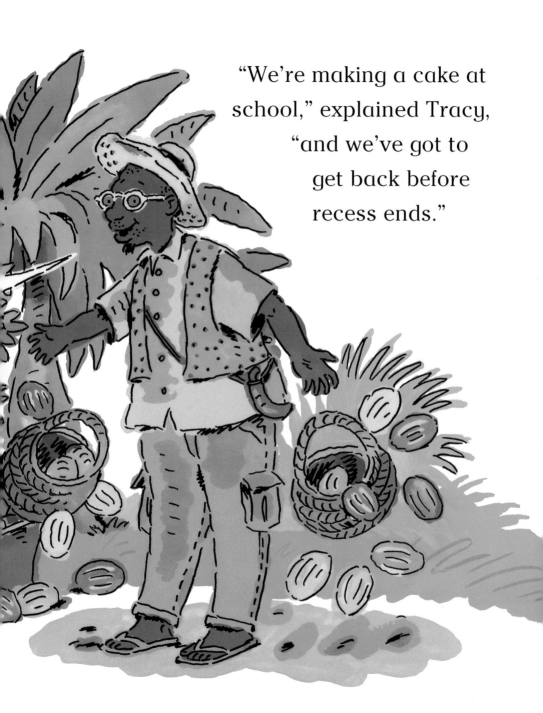

"We're making a cake at school," explained Tracy, "and we've got to get back before recess ends."

31

Uncle William laughed.
He thought they were joking.
"Well, there are the cocoa
trees," he said, pointing to
some tall trees.

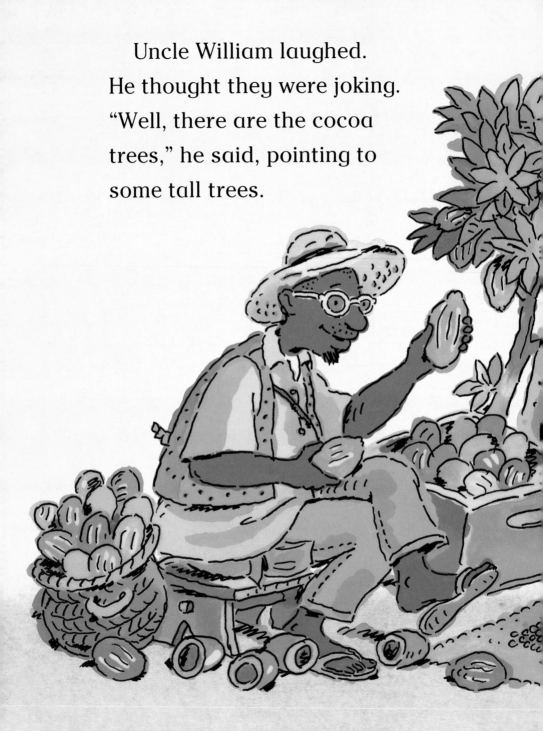

"See the cocoa beans in the big red and yellow pods. See them drying in the sun."

Tracy tugged Josh's arm.
"Josh, we've got to get back
to bake the cake."

Uncle William laughed again and drove
them to the cocoa factory.

When they got to the factory there were
thousands of candy bars, and piles of
cocoa. Uncle William filled the backpack with
cocoa and candy bars. "Now you can
bake that delicious
chocolate cake,"
he said.

"Thank you!" said Josh. He pulled hard on the strings of his magic backpack and . . .

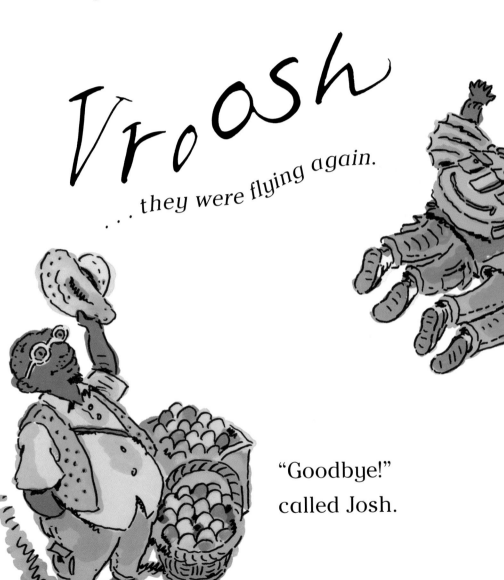

Vroosh

. . . they were flying again.

"Goodbye!" called Josh.

They flew back to school . . .

. . . and arrived just as recess was ending. "Where have you two been?" asked Mrs. Crumble.

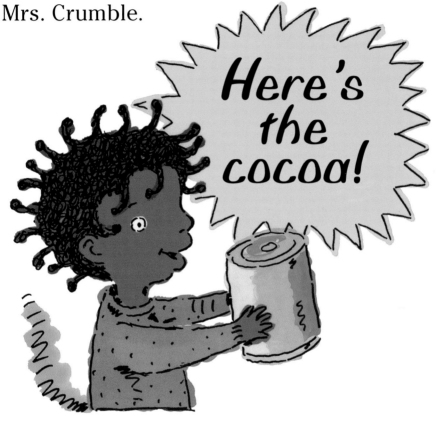

"To get the cocoa," said Josh.

"And the chocolate," said Tracy.

They didn't say they had been to Africa. She wouldn't have believed them.

Everyone helped make the cake. They mixed butter and sugar and eggs and flour and cocoa. Then they put it in the oven.

While it baked, they melted the chocolate.
Then they mixed the chocolate with butter
and icing sugar to make the delicious topping.

When the cake was ready, they iced it and piled it high with chocolate flakes. Their Super-Duper Round the World Chocolate Cake was delicious!

Super-Duper
Round the World
Chocolate Cake
Recipe

When you see this sign, get an adult to help you.

To make the CAKE

You will need:
- 1 3/4 cup (170 g) self-rising flour
- 6 ounces (170 g) soft butter
- 3/4 cup (170 g) sugar
- 1 level teaspoon (5 mL) baking powder
- 3 eggs
- 3 level tablespoons (45 mL) cocoa powder
- 4 tablespoons (60 mL) warm water

1. Sift the flour and baking powder into a bowl.

2. Add the butter, sugar, and eggs.

4. Beat the mixture with a wooden spoon for a few minutes, then with an electric mixer for one minute.

3. Blend the cocoa powder with the warm water. Add to the bowl.

5. Pre-heat the oven to 320°F (160°C).

6. Pour the mixture into a cake pan and bake for 40-45 minutes.

To make the
TOPPING

You will need:
2 1/8 cups (240 g)
  icing sugar
7/8 cup (100 g) dark
  chocolate
1/8 cup (30 g) butter
3 tablespoons (45 mL)
  hot water

1. Put the dark chocolate
   and butter in a bowl.

2. Melt them by
   placing the
   bowl in a pot
   of hot water.

3. Gradually beat in the
   icing sugar and water
   until it is shiny.

4. Spread the
   topping over the
   cake and decorate
   with chocolate
   flakes.

Julia Jarman

Where did you get the idea for this story? I know a little boy called Josh, whose grandparents come from West Africa. He has a backpack and one day I wondered – what if it were magic?

If you had a magic backpack like Josh, where would you go? I would go to Africa!

What is your favorite food? I'm tempted to say chocolate because I like it so much, but I love food of all sorts. And I love trying new things!

How long did it take to write this story? It's hard to say exactly how long it took to write this story, because I thought of the idea and wrote a bit, and then got stuck, and then wrote a bit more, and so on. Then I sent it to an editor who said, "I like it but . . ." She suggested some changes, so I wrote it again!

Can I be a writer like you? Yes, you can! I have a Writing Recipe for cooking up stories. You can try it too.

Adriano Gon

What did you use to paint the pictures in this book? I used wall paint on film. First, I drew the black outlines on the film. Then I added the colors on the back side of the film. You can try it, too.

What would you do if you had a magic backpack? I would go wandering to all kinds of places, like Josh, until supper.

Where do you live? I live in Trieste on the east side of Italy, very close to Venice and by the Slovenian and Croatian border.

What's your favorite food? I like Chinese, Indian, and Italian food. I love to cook. My specialty is homemade green tagliatelle in spicy clam sauce. I really like to eat with all my friends, around a big table.

What's your favorite place to draw? The bathtub.

What did you like to do when you were a child? What did you hate most? I liked to draw people from my village and roller skate. I hated doctors and needles.

Let your ideas take flight with

Flying Foxes

Digging for Dinosaurs
by Judy Waite and Garry Parsons

Only Tadpoles Have Tails
by Jane Clarke and Jane Gray

The Magic Backpack
by Julia Jarman and Adriano Gon

Slow Magic
by Pippa Goodhart and John Kelly

Sherman Swaps Shells
by Jane Clarke and Ant Parker

That's Not Right!
by Alan Durant and Katharine McEwen